John Henry Belville

A Manual of the Barometer

SALZWASSER
VERLAG

John Henry Belville

A Manual of the Barometer

Reprint of the original.

1st Edition 2023 | ISBN: 978-3-37514-774-7

Verlag (Publisher): Salzwasser Verlag GmbH, Zeilweg 44, 60439 Frankfurt, Deutschland
Vertretungsberechtigt (Authorized to represent): E. Roepke, Zeilweg 44, 60439 Frankfurt, Deutschland
Druck (Print): Books on Demand GmbH, In de Tarpen 42, 22848 Norderstedt, Deutschland

A MANUAL

OF

THE BAROMETER;

CONTAINING AN EXPLANATION OF THE

CONSTRUCTION AND METHOD OF USING THE MERCURIAL
BAROMETER, WITH APPROPRIATE TABLES FOR
CORRECTIONS FOR TEMPERATURE, AND RULES FOR
OBTAINING THE DEW-POINT AND THE
HEIGHTS OF MOUNTAINS:

TO WHICH ARE ADDED,

AN ORIGINAL TABLE OF THE MEAN OF THE HEIGHT BAROMETER
FOR EVERY DAY OF THE YEAR, AND PHÆNOMENA OF THE
WINDS AND CLOUDS IN THEIR CONNEXION WITH
THE CHANGES OF THE WEATHER:

ALSO,

A DESCRIPTION OF THE ANEROID BAROMETER.

BY JOHN HENRY BELVILLE,

OF THE ROYAL OBSERVATORY, GREENWICH.

THIRD EDITION.

LONDON:

TAYLOR AND FRANCIS,

RED LION COURT, FLEET STREET.

1858.

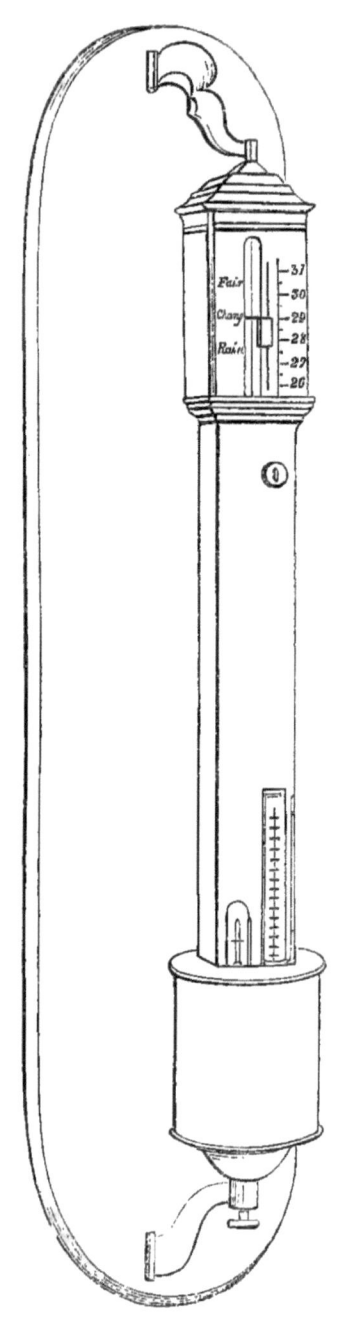

PREFACE.

In the preliminary Chapter on the Atmosphere I have referred to De Luc's 'Recherches sur l'Atmosphère,' Robertson on the Atmosphere, and Dalton's Essays. The barometric table of the mean height of the mercurial column for every day in the year is, I believe, the first of the kind that has been deduced; it is the result of thirty years' observations, made by myself in one locality. In the name of "Henry" my table of daily mean temperatures was used for two or three years, at the Royal Observatory, as a standard of comparison for the temperatures in the weekly report of the Registrar-General, and it was only discontinued when the establishment had accumulated sufficient data from which to deduce a standard of their own: that public acknowledgement of confidence in the accuracy of those results, together with my

professional character as an observer, will give
the value of authenticity to the Table now
published.   The phænomena of the winds and
clouds, in their connexion with the movements
of the barometer, though deduced from observation and experience, are not set forth as
dogmas, but as helps, for the interpretation of
the meteorological appearances of our very
irregular and unsettled climate.   The nomenclature of the clouds is Luke Howard's, by whom,
when a young observer, I was favoured with a
presentation copy of his valuable work on the
Climate of London.

J. H. B.

Hyde Vale, Greenwich, April 1849.

ON

THE ATMOSPHERE.

———◆———

THE Barometer is an instrument for measuring the
weight of the atmosphere; it was invented in 1643 by
Torricelli, who in investigating the cause of water ascending in pumps to the height of 32 feet, and no higher,
made the following experiment. He took a glass tube
about four feet long, sealed at one end and open at the
other, and having filled it with mercury closed the open
end with his finger; he then inverted the tube, and
placed the open end under the surface of a small quantity of mercury in a basin, and raising the tube perpendicular withdrew his finger; he observed the mercury
in the tube suspended to the height of $27\frac{1}{2}$ inches,
above the surface of that in the basin: he compared
the height of the column of mercury with the height of
the column of water raised by the pump, and perceiving
those heights to be in an inverse ratio of the specific
gravities of the water and mercury, he concluded they
were kept in suspension by a common cause; a further
consideration of the experiment led him to remark that
the upper extremities of the columns of water and mercury had no communication with the atmosphere, but
that the lower extremities had a communication, and he

B

attributed the elevation of the columns in the tubes to the weight of the atmosphere.

The curious may amuse themselves with the action of the weight of the atmosphere in the following manner:— Take a glass tube of uniform bore, open at both ends; fit a cork to it, and cement a wire into the cork, which will form a piston to the tube; place the piston even with the lower end of the tube; and in that situation place the same end of the tube in mercury; hold the tube steadily and pull up the piston; the mercury will follow the piston, and will fill that part of the tube which is below the piston. By this means the weight of the atmosphere is removed from off the mercury, which is forced into the tube as far as the piston, by the weight of the atmosphere on the rest of the surface of the mercury in the basin; when the mercury in the tube balances the weight of the atmosphere, it remains stationary; and on pulling the piston higher, the space between it and the mercury is called a vacuum, or space void of air.

In 1646 Pascal at Rouen repeated Torricelli's experiments with similar results. He also varied them by employing liquids of different specific gravities, and he perceived that the lighter the liquid the higher it ascended in the tube; but the agency of an invisible fluid was still doubted, and he therefore determined to make an experiment on the top of the mountain Puy de Dome, near Clermont in Auvergne, which should silence controversy. Two tubes filled with mercury, the columns of equal heights, were carried to the foot of the mountain, one of which was left there standing at 28 inches, and the other taken to the summit; as they ascended, the mercury in the tube gradually sunk until it stood at

24·7 inches; as they descended, the mercury as gradually rose again; and when placed by the side of the tube left below, their elevations coincided. As Pascal had anticipated, in ascending the mountain the weight of a portion of the column of the atmosphere equal to the height of the mountain being removed from the surface of the mercury in the bason, that which was in the tube fell, until its weight was again counterpoised by the atmosphere; and conversely in descending, the weight of the column of the atmosphere being increased by the weight of the portion equal to the height of the mountain, pressed upon the mercury in the basin, and forced it to ascend in the tube until both weights balanced each other.

Pascal originated the idea of measuring elevations by the variations of the barometer, but he foresaw a difficulty. He compared the atmosphere to a mass of wool, the lowest parts of which were more pressed than those above; and his sagacity led him to the fact, that from the dilatation of the atmosphere the rise and fall of the mercurial column would not be equal through equal spaces. This concluded his philosophical inquiries; he afterwards turned his attention to theology.

In 1666 Boyle discovered that the atmosphere was elastic and compressible; and about the same period Mariotte proved its density was in proportion to the weight with which it was compressed. The stratum of the atmosphere nearest the surface of the earth supports the weight of all above it, and is the densest; each stratum as we ascend becomes lighter or more rare, because its elasticity is less checked by having a less weight pressing from above. Père Cotte deduced, that the ratio of the decrease of its density was in geometrical progression, if we take the heights in arithmetical progression. Thus, if the density at 1 mile high was 1, and that at 4 miles high $\frac{1}{2}$, then that at 7 miles high would be $\frac{1}{4}$, at 10 miles high $\frac{1}{8}$, at 13 miles high $\frac{1}{16}$, &c.; but this ratio is much disturbed by changes in the temperature of the strata of the atmosphere at different elevations. Heat expands the bulk of air, and forces it to occupy a larger space; 1000 volumes of air at 32° of Fahrenheit become expanded into 1057·34 volumes at 60°; thus heat is a cause of the unequal rise and fall of the barometer through equal spaces. Sir George Shuckburgh made numerous experiments upon the effects of temperature on the atmosphere; and from his labours we have a table, which shows in feet how much the spaces passed through may vary from temperature in a fall of $\frac{1}{10}$th of an inch of mercury, the barometer standing at 30 inches; and by means of his theorem for its application, we are now enabled to ascertain the heights of mountains by the barometer as correctly as by geometrical measurement.

There exists at all times in the atmosphere a certain portion of vapour, which exerts an influence, varying according to circumstances, upon the mercurial column; it is derived from the spontaneous evaporation of water from the surface of the earth, and is called *aqueous vapour*. Evaporation is promoted by dry air, by wind, by a diminished pressure, and by heat; the *quantity* evaporated is dependent upon temperature; for heat expanding the gaseous portion of the atmosphere, the spaces between its particles are enlarged and their capacities for containing moisture augmented. Aqueous vapour is highly elastic; its elasticity, which increases with an increase of temperature, has been determined by

Dalton, and its force measured by the height of the mercurial column it is capable of supporting. Aqueous vapour, raised at 32° of Fahrenheit, exerts a pressure on the mercury equal to 0·2 of an inch, at 80° to 1·03 inch, at 180° to 15·0 inches, and at 212° to 30·0 inches, —a pressure equal to the pressure of the whole atmosphere at the level of the sea. The quantity of vapour existing in the atmosphere is measured by an Hygrometer. The one now in general use consists of two thermometers, one bulb of which being covered with muslin and kept constantly moist, will, according to the quantity of evaporation at the time of observation, stand lower than the other bulb, which being left free gives the temperature of the air: from the difference of the readings of the two thermometers, we are able by a very simple rule to obtain the *dew-point,* or that degree of the thermometer to which the temperature of the air must fall for the atmosphere to become saturated with the quantity of vapour then actually existing in it, as will be shown by the following example:—

Let free thermometer ... $= 63$ $63 =$ temp. by free therm.
Wet thermometer ...... $= 54$ $16·2$

Difference................. $= 9$ $46·8 =$ dew-point:
Factor to multiply difference ....} $= 1·8$

*By Table 0·337 of an inch $=$ elasticity of vapour in atmosphere.

$16·2 =$ number of degrees to be subtracted from free therm.

If the readings of the two thermometers be alike, the temperature of the *dew-point* will be the same as the temperature of the air; and the air will then be saturated with moisture.

It is chiefly in the nights, and early in the mornings of the winter months, that the atmosphere is saturated

* Page 36.

with vapour, or that vapour is at its *maximum* of elasticity for the temperature. In our climate, vapour never attains its greatest elasticity at a high temperature; for if in the summer months the atmosphere becomes saturated, it is caused by a declension of the heat, which, contracting the spaces between the particles of the air, squeezes the vapour contained in them closer, and thus brings its elasticity to a maximum for the temperature to which the air has fallen. It was upon the changes of temperature in the atmosphere that Dr. James Hutton founded his theory of rain. He considered rain to be formed by the mixture of two strata of the atmosphere of different temperatures, and each saturated with moisture. The mean quantity of the vapour contained by the two strata before the mixture being more than the mean heat of the two (after the combination) can contain, the excess is precipitated :—

			in.
Let temp. of one stratum $= 65°$	its tension or elasticity	$=$	0·617*
Let temp. of the other... $= 41$	...	...	0·274
2|106			0·891
Mean temperature after combination .... } 53	Mean tension after combination...... }		0·446

By Table, the tension of vapour at 53° is 0·414 inch. Therefore vapour of the tension of 0·032 inch of the mercurial column is precipitated in cloud, fog or rain.

Heat and moisture are the principal causes of the variations in the weight of the atmosphere, and necessarily of the variations in the barometer; the moon is considered to have some influence; but if she exert any power in causing accumulations or tides in the atmosphere, her action on the barometer, computed to be about $\frac{1}{100}$th of an inch, is so small, that even with the

* Table, p. 36.

most delicate instruments and the most accurate observers we can scarcely hope to demonstrate it satisfactorily.

The variations of the barometer are less within the
tropics than in the temperate and polar regions; they
vary in different countries in the same latitude, and they
are great in mountainous countries and islands; in Peru
the range of the mercury is about $\frac{1}{3}$rd of an inch, in London $2\frac{1}{2}$ inches, and in St. Petersburg it exceeds 3 inches.

The pressure of the atmosphere at the level of the
sea, the barometer at 30 inches, is 15 lbs. on the square
inch, which amounts to 2160 lbs., or nearly a ton, upon
every square foot. We cannot therefore be surprised at
the effects of so elastic and compressible a body as air,
when it is set in motion; the soft breeze of summer and
the furious hurricane of winter are instances of the effects
of its different velocities.

*On the Construction and Method of Using the Mercurial
Barometer.*

There are various forms of the Barometer, but the
one best suited for meteorological observations consists
of a tube about 33 inches in length, the extremity of
which is inserted into a small reservoir or cistern; and
in order to maintain the mercury in the cistern always
at the same level, the cistern is constructed partly of
leather; that by means of a screw at the bottom, the
surface of the mercury in it may be so adjusted, as to
have it always at the place from which the scale com-
mences. Some barometers are furnished with a gauge
or float, that in great elevations and depressions the
observer may perceive when the mercury in the cistern
sinks too low or rises too high.

Let $a\,b$, fig. 1, be the glass tube plunged into the mercury in the cistern C, and D the surface-line of the fluid in the cistern level with the commencement of the scale, and adjusted to the particular height of the mercury in the tube, which has been actually measured from the surface of the cistern, in the construction of the instrument (which height is called its neutral point): ✓ when the mercury rises in the tube, a portion equal to that rise leaves the cistern, and the surface-line falls towards the dotted line e; and being lower than the surface from which its neutral point was measured, the actual variation in the atmosphere is indicated too little: turn the screw f until the lines on the float h coincide, and the mercury then records the exact change: when depressions occur, the mercury sinking from the tube into the cistern raises the surface-line towards g; in this case the screw f must be unscrewed until the leather at the bottom of the cistern be sufficiently loosened to allow the mercury to assume its proper level at the surface D.

When there is not a gauge to the barometer, the relative capacities of the cistern and tube are ascertained by experiment, in the construction of the instrument, and marked thereon; as is also its neutral point. In this case, when the mercury in the tube is above the neutral point, the difference between it and the neutral point is to be divided by the *capacity,* and the quotient *added* to the observed height will give the correct height; if the mercury be below the neutral point, the difference is to be *divided* as before,

Fig. 1.

and the quotient *subtracted* from the observed height will give the correct height.

Let capacity for every inch of elevation of the mercury in the tube be equal to $\frac{1}{40}$, which, reduced to a decimal, will be

in.   in.   in.
= 0·025 for 1 inch., 0·013 for $\frac{1}{2}$ inch, 0·007 for $\frac{1}{4}$ inch.

	in.			in.
Observed height...	= 30·400		Observed height.........	29·500
Neutral point......	= 30·000		Neutral point............	30·000
Difference above } neutral point }	·400		Difference below neu-} tral point ....}	·500
Add for capacity ...+	·010		Subtract for capacity	− ·013
Correct height......	30·410		Correct height	29·487

The scale of the standard barometer used in fixed observatories is made moveable, and terminates in an ivory point, which is brought down to the surface of the mercury: when this point and its reflexion appear to touch one another, the height indicated is correct. This kind of barometer requires no adjustment or correction for the cistern.

The tubes of barometers vary in size: those of a large diameter are preferable, as the motion of the fluid is freer, and its friction against the sides of the tube is nearly inappreciable; tubes of small diameters require correction for capillarity, or the depression of the mercury caused by its adhesion to the sides of the tube.

The range of the barometer, or the spaces passed through by the mercury in its extreme depressions and elevations, being limited to $3\frac{1}{2}$ inches, it is not usual to graduate the scale from the lower end of the tube: the divisions commence at 27 inches, and are continued to 31 inches. The graduations on Troughton's mountain barometers for measuring great elevations, commence at 15 inches and are carried on to 33 inches. Each inch is divided into ten equal parts, and these parts are subdivided into hundredths by means of a Vernier (so named from Peter Vernier, its inventor). The Vernier (A, figs. 2 & 3) is a moveable plate, one inch and one-tenth of an inch (together equal to $\frac{11}{10}$) in length; these eleven-tenths are divided into ten equal parts, each part being equal to one-tenth of an inch and one-tenth of a tenth, together equal to eleven hundredths. When the pointer of the Vernier coincides with a division of the barometer scale, as in fig. 2, each division of the Vernier will exceed each division of the scale respectively by 1, 2, 3, 4, 5, 6, 7, 8, 9, 10 parts, whose denominators are the number of parts between a, b; the excess of each division being $\frac{1}{10}$ of a tenth or $\frac{1}{100}$, $\frac{2}{10}$ of a tenth or $\frac{2}{100}$, $\frac{3}{10}$ of a tenth or $\frac{3}{100}$, $\frac{4}{10}$ of a tenth or $\frac{4}{100}$, &c. The pointer in this position reads off to inches and tenths, viz. thirty inches and one tenth, expressed in figures 30·10 inches.

When the *pointer* does *not* coincide with a division of the scale as in fig. 3, observe which division of the Vernier does coincide; and the number placed against that division of the Vernier will be the number of hundredths to be added to the inches and tenths. In fig. 3, 7 coincides with a division of the barometer scale, and therefore 7 hundredths are to be added to the inches and tenths, and the reading is thirty inches, one tenth and seven hundredths, expressed in figures 30·17 inches. By an alteration in the divisions of the Vernier, the mountain and standard barometer are read off to $\frac{1}{500}$th of an inch.

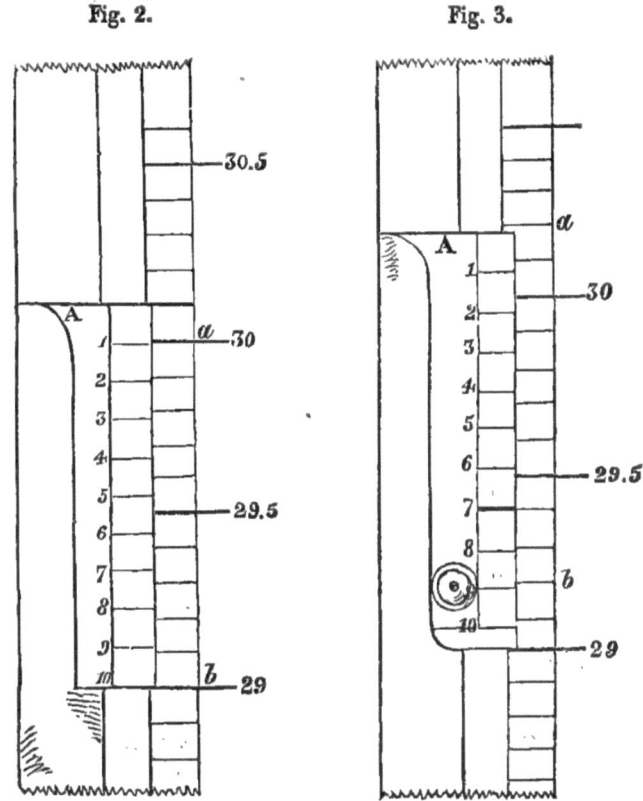

Fig. 2. Fig. 3.

A thermometer is attached to the barometer to indicate the temperature of the mercury in the cistern; all
bodies expand by heat and contract with cold; the expansion of mercury is easily tested by exposing a mercurial thermometer to the heat of a fire, or by placing
it in hot water: as the warmth increases, the mercury
will expand and ascend in the tube; as it diminishes,
it will contract and fall towards the bulb: if the thermometer be plunged into a mixture of pounded ice and
common salt, from the intense cold produced by the
conversion of the ice into water, the mercury will sink

to zero, or 32° below the freezing-point of Fahrenheit; if the tube of the thermometer should not be long enough to admit of so low a graduation, the mercury will shrink into the bulb. The expansion of mercury is $\frac{1}{9990}$ of its bulk for each degree of Fahrenheit between 32° and 212°. For convenience, tables have been computed, from which may be taken out, at sight, the amount to be subtracted from the height of the mercurial column, on account of the expansion of the mercury from temperature.

The words Change, Fair, and Rain, engraved on the plate of the barometer, were placed there by the first observers of its variations: no great importance should be attached to them; for from the observations of two centuries we find, that heavy rains, and of long continuance, take place with the mercury at 29·5 inches or Change; that rain frequently falls when it stands as high as 30·00 inches, or Fair; and, more particularly in winter, a fine bright day will succeed a stormy night, the mercury ranging as low as 29·00 inches, or opposite to Rain. It is not so much the *absolute* height as the actual rising and falling of the mercury which determines the kind of weather likely to follow. The late great elevation of 30·9 inches in February of the present year 1849, was succeeded by a minimum of 29·25 inches, which produced a storm of wind so violent that the horizontal pressure of many of the gusts amounted to 20 lbs. upon the square foot; a pressure which is rarely exceeded, even when the barometer falls as low as 28·25 inches. This may appear extraordinary if we merely take into consideration the actual height of the column, and neglect the *quantity* of the fall which amounted to 1·65 inch. The mean height of the greatest observed elevations for the last thirty-eight years is 30·61 inches, and the mean height of the observed depressions for the same period is 28·69 inches; therefore a fall in the mercury of 1·65 inch from the mean of the elevations would give a *minimum* of 28·96 inches; a depression which is contemporary with violent storms, as it is within three-tenths of the mean of the lowest depressions of the barometer.

In fixing the barometer great care must be taken to fix it perpendicular: a situation should be selected subject to the least change of temperature, for which reason a northern aspect is preferable to a southern; the height of the cistern of the barometer above the level of the sea, and, if possible, the difference of the height of the mercury with some standard, should be ascertained, in order that the observations made with it should be comparative with others made in different parts of the country. Before taking an observation, the instrument should be gently tapped to prevent any adhesion of the mercury to the tube, the gauge should be adjusted to the surface-line of the cistern, and the index of the Vernier brought level with the top of the mercury. If the barometer have a Vernier which admits the light from behind, the lower part of the pointer must make a tangent with the convex part of the mercury in the tube. In reading off the observation the eye should be on a line with the mercury; as by placing it above, the reading would be too low, and by placing it below, it would be too high. This difference in the manner of reading off is called error from parallax. It is indispensable that a reading of the attached thermometer be made simultaneously with the observation of the height of the mercury. Accuracy is the spirit of observation. A careful reading of inches, tenths and hundredths produces excellent results: the

$\frac{1}{1000}$ place is better left to the skill of the old observer who is usually obliged to estimate it, scarcely any barometer being graduated with sufficient precision to trust to the divisions for so small a quantity.

The barometer is slightly affected periodically during the twenty-four hours: at 9 A.M. and 9 P.M. it stands higher, and at 3 A.M. and 3 P.M. it stands lower; the mean annual difference amounts nearly to ·03 of an inch. These four periods of the day have been recommended for observation by the Committee of Physics of the Royal Society. It is usual, for the sake of comparison, to reduce the observations to 32° of Fahrenheit.

Ex. If barom. stood at 29·900 therm. attached 54°,
  Correct for temp.   —·057 (by Table),

Height of barom. at temp. of 32° ...} 29·843

The wheel-barometer, from its construction, cannot be trusted to for correct heights; it merely shows if the mercury be in a rising or falling state: it may rather be considered as an ornamental piece of furniture than as having the slightest pretensions to a scientific instrument.

Mean height of the Barometer at noon for Greenwich, Kent, for every day of the year, deduced from thirty consecutive years' observations, viz. from 1815 to 1844, and reduced to 32° Fahrenheit. Assumed elevation 60 feet above the level of the Sea.

Day of the month.	January.	February.	March.	April.	May.	June.	July.	August.	Sept.	October.	Nov.	Dec.	Day of the month.
	in.	in.	in.	in.	in.	in.	in.	in.	in.	in.	in.	in.	
1.	29·987	29·831	29·763	29·909	29·881	29·941	29·921	29·945	29·881	29·747	29·814	29·778	1.
2.	·997	·748	·791	·843	·876	·904	·918	·928	·919	·834	·816	·789	2.
3.	·971	·851	·774	·915	·834	·879	·915	·869	·928	·902	·789	·839	3.
4.	·892	·907	·766	·944	·815	·855	·925	·826	·913	·896	·793	·846	4.
5.	·964	·886	·828	·959	·819	·860	·902	·862	·904	·907	·785	·909	5.
6.	·977	·919	·796	·873	·822	·912	·903	·868	·860	·897	·782	·868	6.
7.	·981	·851	·739	·835	·859	·939	·899	·904	·852	·863	·794	·839	7.
8.	30·020	·911	·777	·852	·861	·911	·874	·902	·805	·875	·833	·809	8.
9.	30·014	·924	·821	·847	·864	·914	·912	·886	·843	·883	·764	·869	9.
10.	29·876	·954	·866	·882	·889	·917	·926	·869	·844	·875	·802	·927	10.
11.	30·107	·964	·869	·848	·908	·935	·865	·884	·896	·836	·846	·950	11.
12.	·885	·937	·903	·774	·878	·964	·849	·925	·896	·851	·801	·928	12.
13.	·806	·963	·901	·951	·838	·934	·871	·888	·922	·917	·744	·919	13.
14.	·819	·904	·924	·878	·862	·895	·887	·909	·893	·925	·756	·962	14.
15.	·863	·936	·893	·884	·857	·887	·874	·822	·881	·924	·739	·943	15.
16.	·897	·897	·931	·817	·856	·934	·937	·884	·887	·868	·879	·885	16.
17.	·920	·864	·944	·851	·888	·930	·939	·927	·917	·842	·917	·825	17.
18.	·956	·887	·996	·872	·867	·893	·827	·919	·889	·893	·944	·745	18.
19.	·889	·846	·938	·925	·898	·901	·821	·921	·929	·863	·906	·851	19.
20.	·885	·811	·977	·911	·882	·885	·804	·893	·912	·822	·783	·815	20.
21.	·890	·811	·879	·861	·917	·895	·846	·892	·840	·874	·746	·874	21.
22.	·865	·865	·831	·800	·939	·884	·899	·884	·840	·838	·761	·891	22.
23.	·889	·841	·804	·745	·944	·900	·896	·889	·839	·764	·797	·851	23.
24.	·903	·789	·807	·797	·895	·893	·922	·904	·809	·734	·839	·815	24.
25.	·922	·789	·814	·888	·877	·905	·955	·908	·858	·774	·899	·868	25.
26.	·876	·761	·867	·902	·848	·904	·957	·914	·875	·813	·858	·907	26.
27.	·899	·702	·914	·879	·921	·920	·984	·925	·839	·814	·737	·890	27.
28.	·869	29·802	·846	·889	·936	·911	·912	·894	·848	·844	·655	·934	28.
29.	·898	......	·880	·838	·947	·956	·861	·892	·789	·863	29·745	·992	29.
30.	·866	......	·902	29·832	·964	29·955	29·821	·894	29·821	·838		·997	30.
31.	·881	......	·832		29·957		29·889	29·865		29·808		·979	31.
Means.	29·909	29·859	29·857	29·865	29·884	29·910	29·894	29·890	29·872	29·851	29·801	29·884	Means.

The foregoing Table of the daily mean heights of the barometer for Greenwich for every day of the year is the result of thirty years' observations made in one locality, and, with few exceptions for so long a period, by one person. The instrument by which the greater number were registered is by Watkins and Hill, the tube of which has a bore $\frac{6}{10}$ths of an inch in diameter. The Table is original, and it may assist in confirming that, at certain seasons of the year, great periodic atmospheric *maxima* and *minima* take place. The greatest daily mean pressure for the year, which a consecutive five years' observations will not only verify but increase, occurs about the 9th of January, and the minimum daily mean depression towards the end of November. It is a remarkable co-incidence, that the lowest daily mean temperature for thirty years occurs on the 8th and 9th of January, and the daily mean temperature for November rises suddenly four degrees in the last few days in November.

The greatest monthly mean pressure occurs in June, and the lowest in November.

From June the monthly mean pressure declines till November, when it again rises and attains a second maximum in January; and again falling, comes to its second minimum in March.

The mean annual pressure for noon at Greenwich is 29·872 inches.

A Table of the greatest and least observed heights of the Barometer for the last thirty-eight years, taken at Greenwich, and reduced to 32° of Fahrenheit.

Date of the year.	Greatest observed height of barometer.	Least observed height of barometer.	Greatest annual range.	Date of the year.	Greatest observed height of barometer.	Least observed height of barometer.	Greatest annual range.
	in.	in.	in.		in.	in.	in.
1811.	30·46	28·68	1·78	1830.	30·63	28·61	2·02
1812.	30·55	28·50	2·05	1831.	30·58	28·93	1·65
1813.	30·47	28·65	1·82	1832.	30·64	29·12	1·52
1814.	30·40	28·21	2 19	1833.	30·71	28·77	1·94
1815.	30·63	28·86	1·77	1834.	30·66	29·13	1·53
1816.	30·67	28·72	1 95	1835.	30·84	28·74	2·10
1817.	30·63	28·51	2·12	1836.	30·69	28·62	2·07
1818.	30·62	28·54	2·08	1837.	30·68	28·77	1·91
1819.	30·52	29·11	1·41	1838.	30·58	28·61	1·97
1820.	30·75	28·67	2·08	1839.	30·57	28·97	1·60
1821.	30·82	27·99	2·83	1840.	30·68	28·59	2·09
1822.	30·70	29·11	1·59	1841.	30·49	28·82	1·67
1823.	30·62	28·60	2·02	1842.	30·58	28·69	1·89
1824.	30·57	28·46	2·11	1843.	30·54	28·20	2·34
1825.	30·89	28·74	2·15	1844.	30·53	28·63	1·90
1826.	30·57	28·80	1·77	1845.	30·57	28·77	1·80
1827.	30·70	28·77	1·93	1846.	30·66	28·66	2·00
1828.	30 55	28·92	1·63	1847.	30·53	28·48	2·05
1829.	30·59	28·92	1·67	1848.	30·48	28·40	2·08

In the preceding Table the *maximum* elevation for the period of thirty-eight years occurred in 1825, when the mercury stood at 30·89 inches; in 1821 it however reached 30·82 inches; in 1835, 30·84 inches; and in February 1849, 30·86 inches. It is recorded that Sir George Shuckburgh, in 1778 in London, observed the barometer at 30·935 inches, which he believed to be the greatest elevation ever seen.

In the extreme depressions, those of 1821 and 1843 differ only by 21 hundredths: the first occurred on the 25th of December, when a Troughton's mountain-barometer at the Royal Observatory sunk as low as 27·89 inches. (See Pond's 'Greenwich Astronomical Observations, 1821.') A heavy rain of some hours' duration, with the wind at south-east, had preceded the minimum pressure; a gale from the north-west followed, in which the mercury rose a few tenths.

The depression of 1814, 28·21 inches, happened at the close of the great frost, and was likewise preceded by a stormy wind from south-south-east and much rain.

The difference of the extremes of the elevations is 0·49 inch.

The difference of the extremes of the depressions is 1·14 inch.

The following is the progress of the great depression of January 13, 1843.

Hour of the day.	Height of the barom.	State of the weather.
2 A.M.	in. 29·02	Sky overcast with cirro-stratus: ground covered with snow. Temperature 30°.
5.	28·72	Rain and Wind. Direction S.
7.	28·54	Wind unusually violent.
8.	28·48	
8·45.	28·41	Dense nimbi. Thunder and lightning. } Wind
9·15.	28·40	Dense nimbi. Rain and Wind. } S.S.W.
10.	28·37	Tremendous squalls.
11.	28·34	Showers of rain discharged horizontally from
Noon.	28·30	nimbi.
1 P.M.	28·23	Wind blowing a hurricane from S.W.
2.	28 29	More moderate.
3.	28·34	
4·30.	28·37	Wind as violent as before, blowing down trees.
6.	28·48	Direction of wind W.
10.	28·68	Steady heavy gale from W. with scud. Temp. 38°·5.

The horizontal pressure of the most violent gusts was 20 and 25 lbs. on the square foot, the wind having a velocity of 60 and 80 miles an hour.

It may be proper to observe, that neither *extreme* elevations nor *extreme* depressions occur suddenly, the mercury being usually for some few days preceding them in a gradually rising or falling state.

A Table showing the age, declination, and position of the Moon in her orbit, in some of the most remarkable elevations of the Barometer.

Date of the year.	Day of the month.	Height of the barometer.	Moon's age.	Moon's declination.	Position of the Moon in her orbit.
		in.	days	°	
1816.	Dec. 1.	30·67	14	11 N.	Apogee.
1820.	Jan. 9.	30·75	25	15 S.	Mean.
1821.	Feb. 6.	30·82	5	10 N.	Perigee.
1822.	Feb. 28.	30·70	8	27 N.	Perigee.
1825.	Jan. 9.	30·89	22	Equator.	Perigee.
1827.	Dec. 28.	30·70	10	20 N.	Apogee.
1833.	Jan. 8.	30·71	18	15 N.	Perigee.
1835.	Jan. 2.	30·84	3	18 S.	Mean.
1836.	Jan. 2.	30·69	14	26 N.	Apogee.
1837.	Oct. 14.	30·68	15	14 N.	Past perigee.
1840.	Mar. 8.	30·68	4	22 N.	Perigee.
1849.	Feb. 11.	30·86	18	Equator.	Mean.

A Table showing the age, declination, and position of the Moon in her orbit, in some of the most remarkable depressions of the Barometer.

Date of the year.	Day of the month.	Height of the barometer.	Moon's age.	Moon's declination.	Position of the Moon in her orbit.
		in.	days	°	
1814.	Jan. 29.	28·21	8	15 N.	Near perigee.
1817.	Dec. 8.	28·51	New.	26 N.	Perigee.
1818.	Mar. 4.	28·54	29	26 S.	Mean.
1821.	Dec. 25.	27·99	3	25 S.	Perigee.
1824.	Nov. 23.	28·46	4	20 S.	Apogee.
1830.	Jan. 20.	28·61	27	17 S.	Past apogee.
1836.	Feb. 2.	28·62	Full.	16 N.	Perigee.
1838.	Nov. 28.	28·61	12	16 N.	Perigee.
1840.	Nov. 13.	28·59	19	24 N.	Past perigee.
1843.	Jan. 13.	28·20	13	24 N.	Mean.
1847.	Dec. 6.	28·48	28	17 S.	Apogee.
1848.	Feb. 26.	28·40	21	16 S.	Apogee.

From these Tables it does not appear that the moon exerts any influence on the extreme movements of the barometer.

Phænomena of the Barometer.

Strong winds in the winter from the west with a steady high pressure, invariably bring a high temperature and very little rain; with winds from the east, a low temperature and sharp frosts.

If the mercury fall during a high wind from the south-west, south-south-west, or west-south-west, an increasing storm is probable; if the fall be rapid, the wind will be violent, but of short duration; if the fall be slow, the wind will be less violent, but of longer continuance; the disturbing cause is probably the same in each case, but its intensity unequal: nearly all our high winds from the south-west come with a falling barometer.

If the depression of the mercury be sudden and considerable with the wind due west, a violent storm may be expected from the north-west or north, during which the mercury will rise to its former height. If the mercury fall with the wind at north-west, or north, a great reduction of temperature will follow; in the winter severe frosts, in the summer cold rains.

A steady and considerable fall of the mercury during an east wind denotes that the wind will soon go round to the south, unless a heavy fall of snow or rain immediately follow; in this case the *upper* clouds usually come up from the south. The deep snow of the severe winter of 1814 was a notable instance.

The lowest depressions occur with the wind at south and south-east, when much rain falls, and frequently short and severe gales blow from these points. In the winter months, sudden depressions of the mercury with the wind in these quarters are attended with electrical phænomena.

A fall of the mercury with a south wind is invariably followed by rain in greater or less quantities.

A falling barometer with the wind at north brings the worst weather: in the summer, rain and storm follow; in the winter and spring, deep snows and severe frosts. This case is of rare occurrence.

A great depression of the mercury during a frosty period brings on a thaw: if the wind be south or south-east, the thaw will continue; if the wind be south-west, the frost will be likely to return with a rising barometer and northerly wind.

In the winter season, a rapid rise of the mercury immediately after a gale from the south-west with rain (the wind going round to north-west or north) is usually attended with clear sky and sharp white frosts.

Great depressions in the summer months are attended with storms of wind and rain with thunder and hail: cold unseasonable weather generally succeeds these depressions.

During a period of broken cold weather in the winter months, with the wind at north or north-north-west, a sudden rise of the mercury denotes the approach of rain and a southerly wind *.

During a steady frost with the wind at north, north-east, or east, a continued slow rising of the mercury indicates snow and cloudy weather.

If the mercury rise with the wind at south-west, south, or even south-east, the temperature is generally high.

Observation does not show that *extremes of temperature* are contemporaneous with the greatest elevations and least depressions of the mercurial column.

Meteors are not prevalent during very low pressures: the *Aurora Borealis* has been noticed at all heights of the barometer. Small flashes of lightning are of frequent occurrence during stormy weather in the winter season when the mercury stands low.

Great elevations in the summer are generally attended with dry, warm weather.

Great depressions at all seasons are followed by change of wind, and by much rain.

A rising barometer with a southerly wind is usually followed by fine weather. In the summer it is dry and warm; in the winter, dry with moderate frosts. This is of rare occurrence.

When the mercury is very unsteady during calm rainy weather, it denotes that the air is in an electrical state, and that thunder will follow.

In the summer months, if a depression of two or three tenths of the mercury occur in a hot period, it is attended with rain and thunder, and succeeded by a cool atmosphere. Sometimes heavy thunder-storms take place overhead without any fall of the mercury; in this case a reduction of temperature does not usually follow.

Rain in some quantity may fall with a high pressure, provided the wind be in any of the northerly points; and when much rain

* Thaws also commonly set in during the night.

falls with a steady rising barometer and the mercury attains a great elevation, a long period of fine weather usually succeeds.

If after a storm of wind and rain, the mercury remain steady at the point to which it had fallen, serene weather may follow without a change of wind; but on the rising of the mercury, rain and a change of wind may be expected.

During a series of stormy weather the mercury is in constant agitation, falling and rising twice or thrice in the space of twenty-four hours, the wind changing alternately from south to west, and backing again to the south: this alternation of winds continues until the mercury rises to a bold elevation, when it ceases, and the weather becomes settled.

Storms of wind, especially when accompanied with much rain, produce the greatest depressions of the mercury. No storm of wind on record has blown without some rain falling, although the time of its falling and its amount have been variable: sometimes the rain has increased with the increasing storm and sinking mercury; at other times the rain has fallen suddenly at the close of the storm, or at the time of the *minimum* pressure.

No great storm ever sets in with a steady rising barometer.

As far as regards the locality of Greenwich, the most violent gusts of wind come from due south, and those next in violence from due north; in both instances the mercury remains stationary at its *minimum* point during the greatest *horizontal pressure*: the winds from these quarters are of short duration, and limited in their extent. The ordinary south-west gales will blow unremittingly for twenty-four hours, and will sweep over the whole of the British Isles.

Note. Although a rising mercury attends a northerly wind, great depressions occur previously to a great storm coming from that quarter.

In England, the winds which blow for the greatest number of days together without intermission, are the west and west-south-west: they blow chiefly during the winter months, and are the principal cause of our mild winters.

The east and east-north-east are the winds the next most prevalent. The great antagonist winds, the north and south, are the origin of our most violent storms.

The westerly winds surge mostly by night, and their average force is twice that of the easterly winds.

The easterly winds are generally calm at night, but blow with some power during the day.

On an average, sunrise and sunset are the periods of the twenty-four hours in which there is the least wind. An hour or two after noon is the period when the wind is the highest.

As a general rule, when the wind turns against the sun, or *retrogrades* from west to south, it is attended with a falling mercury; when it goes in the *same direction* as the sun, or turns direct from west to north, the mercury rises, and there is a probability of fine weather.

It never hails in calm weather. When hail falls, it is during sudden gusts of wind, and the mercury rises while the hail is actually falling.

If the weather during harvest-time has been generally fine, and a fall of the mercury with a shower occur,—if the wind turn a few points to the north and the barometer rises above 30 inches, the weather may be expected to be fair for some days.

The finest and most beneficial state of the atmosphere, more especially as regards the health of man, is with a uniform pressure at a mean height of the climate varying from 29·80 to 30·00.

When there is only one current of air subsisting in the atmosphere, there is seldom much variation in the height of the mercurial column. It is when two or more *strata* of the air are in motion in different directions at the same time, that great fluctuations of the mercury occur.

In high pressures, the *upper* current usually sets from the northward; in low pressures it sets from the south and southwest.

The variations of the barometer are always greater in the winter than in the summer.

In accounting for the different currents of the atmosphere, it must be remarked that the great heat of the torrid zone causes a constant ascent of air over it, which passes northward and southward; while an under current of cold air flows from the poles to supply its place; the diurnal rotation of the earth combined with these currents causes the trade-winds, whose direction is from east to west: these currents would from the same causes become in the north temperate zone north-east and south-west winds, and in the south temperate zone south-east and north-west winds; but the great irregularities of the temperature from the seasons, the large tracts of ocean, and the different geographical formations of the land, subject them to interruptions, and give to every country its prevailing winds, derived from local causes. In England, the south-south-west, south-west, and west-south-west winds set in towards the end of October, and blow with their greatest strength during November, December, and February, and are even powerful in June and July: the winds from the westerly quarters prevail in March, but they then veer more towards the north, whence they blow with great violence: in April, the east and north-east, and the west and north-west winds balance each other, and their comparative strength is nearly equal: in May, the east, north-east, and north-north-east winds preponderate; the latter blows the less frequently, but with the greatest violence; in this month the average of the winds from the westerly quarters ranges low; their average strength also decreases, with the exception of that from the west-south-west, which ranges higher than in April. In August the west and west-south-west winds prevail, but their power is moderate; the stormy winds of this month blow from the west-south-west and north-north-west. September is the calmest period of the year; in this month the north and south winds, and the east and west winds, balance each other; in January the east and west winds upon an average are nearly equal, both as regards the number of times they blow, and their average strength; the winds from the south-south-west, west-south-west, and the north-westerly quarters are more rare, but they blow with great violence. As the winds from these opposite quarters predominate, so is the character of our winters determined as to mildness or severity.

Sudden depressions of the barometer sometimes occur in weather apparently calm. It is almost an established fact that storms have a circular motion; and if, when an exhaustion or sudden diminution of the atmosphere takes place, the mercurial column happen to be in the partial vacuum or centre of motion, the air will be at rest; while the surrounding air at a greater distance from the centre will be violently agitated with a less fall of the barometer. This circular motion of the atmosphere is not confined to one spot where the storm may commence and expend its violence; but it has a progressive cycloidal movement onwards, changing constantly the situation of its centre of motion, and, as it advances, enlarging its circumference, until, having traversed many hundred miles, it becomes exhausted as the air recovers its equilibrium. These great rarefactions of the atmosphere are probably the effects of electricity; they are common in their most terrific form in the Indian Ocean, on the western coast of Africa, and in the West Indies.

In our own climate the approach of thunder-clouds produces violent squalls of wind; and dense and highly electrified clouds will sometimes raise miniature whirlwinds as they pass overhead*.

Of the Clouds.

Howard's Nomenclature.

Cirrus.	Cumulo-Stratus.
Cirro-Stratus.	Stratus.
Cirro-Cumulus.	Nimbus.
Cumulus.	Scud.

The *Cirrus* cloud is seen at all seasons of the year, and at all heights of the barometer. It occupies the most elevated regions of the atmosphere, and is supposed to be above the limit of perpetual congelation (in our *latitude* about 6000 feet). It is easily distinguished from all other clouds by its delicate, fibrous, thread-like, curling or feathery texture; it lies in light patches on the blue sky, sometimes so faintly that the eye can scarcely discern it; its motion is very slow, and in serene weather with a high pressure it will retain its form unaltered for many hours. If the mercury be falling, its changes are rapid; and on the approach of rain its delicate texture becomes confused, and is ultimately lost in one dusky mass, resembling *ground glass*. During these changes the Cirrus has been descending; and its

* The mean annual horizontal pressure of the wind at Greenwich may be estimated at ½lb. on the square foot; equal to a velocity of 10 miles per hour.

peculiar characteristics having disappeared, it assumes a new nomenclature, the Cirro-Stratus. The progressive increase of the Cirrus cloud is generally from the west.

The *Cirro-Stratus* is likewise in the higher regions of the atmosphere, and is seen at all seasons of the year : it is the immediate precursor of rain or wind and of a *falling* barometer. Sometimes it spreads itself over the heavens so attenuated, that the sun, though it shines through it, casts its shadows indistinctly; at other times it spreads itself in lurid darkness, threatening storm and tempest, but terminating in rain or wind. If, after a rapid rise in the mercury, this cloud make its appearance in bars, or streaks which seem to converge in the horizon, rain shortly follows. It is in the Cirro-Stratus cloud that *halos, parhelia, paraselenæ,* &c. are formed.

The *Cirro-Cumulus,* or warm-weather cloud, attends a *rising* barometer. This pretty modification is often formed from the *Cirrus.* The *Cirro-Stratus* will also frequently after rain dissolve into *Cirro-Cumulus,* an indication that the frozen mass of which the *Cirro-Stratus* is formed is thawed on its descent into a warmer atmosphere ; where becoming attenuated, it breaks and splits, leaving clear blue sky between the small round patches of cloud, which take the name of *Cirro-Cumulus.* This cloud is often seen alone in the higher regions ; it then assumes a dappled appearance, or what is popularly called a mackerel-back sky. *Coloured Coronæ* have their origin in this cloud.

The *Cumulus* cloud is seen chiefly in the spring and summer months. Its form, when viewed sideways, increases from above in dense, convex heaps ; in showery weather it is tufted with the Cirro-Stratus, and in the interval of the showers its texture is fleecy and its form changes rapidly. In hot weather it often appears stationary with a flattened base, its rock-like summits shining with a silvery light. If during a fine morning this cloud suddenly disappear, and it be followed by the Cirro-Stratus cloud with the wind backing to the south, the mercury falls, and rain soon follows.

The Cumulus is the day cloud: its great density keeps off the too scorching rays of the noonday sun; it usually evaporates an hour or two before sunset. When it increases *after* sunset, and shines with a ruddy copper-coloured light, it denotes a thunder-storm. The Cumulus frequently attends a rising barometer. The Cumulus is uncommon during the winter months.

The *Cumulo-Stratus* cloud is most frequent in the spring and summer months. It indicates thundergusts, showers of hail and sudden changes of the wind. It is the densest modification of cloud, and as it passes overhead it causes a reduction of temperature. Its form is compounded of the rocky Cumulus, the Cirro-Stratus and Cirro-Cumulus; its texture is puckered or corrugated, and before thunder it becomes deeply fringed, so that it appears to touch the ground. It forms the basis of great thunder-storms, its electrical character attracting clouds and scud from all quarters of the heavens, which uniting confusedly, constitute that indescribable black mass always antecedent to storms of thunder and lightning.

The effect of the Cumulo-Stratus cloud on the mercury appears to be to give it a tendency to rise.

The *Nimbus* is a modification of the Cumulo-Stratus cloud seen in profile during a shower. Its course can be distinctly traced on land, by the dark mist occasioned by the rain then actually falling. The Nimbus is never seen with the barometer at great elevations.

The rainbow is the lovely attendant of the Nimbus cloud *only*.

The *Stratus* is the cloud nearest the ground. It is formed from the sudden chill of certain strata of the atmosphere, which condensing the vapour contained in them, renders it visible in a misty cloud or creeping fog. Calm weather is essential to the formation of the Stratus; it is frequent in fine autumnal nights and mornings, sometimes resting on the ground, sometimes hovering some hundred feet above it. It obscures the sun until his rays have raised the temperature of the air sufficiently to evaporate it, when it gradually disappears and leaves a clear blue sky. The Stratus deposits moisture :- and when the temperature, from radiation or other causes, sinks below 32°, we find it fettered in icy spiculæ upon trees and shrubs, and sparkling in exquisite frostwork upon all nature.

The Stratus is called the night cloud, and is most frequent from September till January. It has no sensible effect on the barometer.

Scud is, with the exception of the *Stratus*, the lowest cloud. It is most commonly seen during the winter months, with every wind that blows and with all pressures of the atmosphere. It always moves in the direction of the wind, and apparently with great rapidity. It is more frequently seen after rain than at any other period. In our westerly gales in winter, it continues for days together, deforming the sky with its large, loose, shapeless masses.

The several modifications of cloud may be separated into two great divisions; the first comprising the Cirrus, Cirrus-Stratus, Cirro-Cumulus, and Scud, which *descend* in the atmosphere; these produce rain, wind, &c., and affect the mercurial column: it is during their progressive movement downwards that the barometer is seen to fall. The second division consisting of the Stratus, which gives place to the Cumulus; they have their origin in the lower strata of the atmosphere, and are the *ascending* clouds; they are the harbingers of fine weather, and have no effect on the movements of the barometer.

It is not uncommon to observe two or three *strata* of clouds moving in different directions; the *lowest* follows the direction of the wind blowing at the time near the surface of the earth; the *upper* strata follow the currents in the upper regions of the atmosphere; which may be in opposite directions. Before thunder and heavy rain this is of usual occurrence, the barometer at the time being low or in a falling state.

In hot sultry weather, especially after a slight fall of the mercury, small clouds sometimes suddenly form on a clear blue sky, and as suddenly vanish; this is a sure sign of electricity. If the clouds collect without any progressive motion and increase rapidly, and a haze be observed *above* the clouds, a storm will in all probability be in the vicinity; but if they move hurriedly towards any particular quarter of the heavens, the storm will be in the direction whither the clouds are seen to hasten: these signs of thunder are seen, though the storm may be 150 miles distant.

Much has been accomplished towards gaining a knowledge of the forms and modifications of the clouds by the classification of Luke Howard. Still, in certain states of the atmosphere, when the clouds mix confusedly and change their forms abruptly, it is difficult for the inexperienced to class them; the prevailing modification of the day, in connexion with the movement of the barometer, is however sufficient to establish the character of the weather.

The splendid crimson contrasting with the delicate azure of a fine autumnal sunset, and the golden flood encroaching upon the deep blue of a summer's sunrise, are chiefly referable to the lofty Cirrus and Cirro-Cumulus clouds. Perhaps no climate in the temperate zone can boast, during the fine period of the year, of clouds of so many beautiful and so varied forms as Great Britain. They are the production of Great Nature's hand, and are anticipated with equal delight by the painter, the meteorologist and the contemplative mind.

A Table showing the average quantity of Rain at Greenwich, Kent, for each month of the year, deduced from thirty-four consecutive years from 1815 to 1848.

Month of the year.	Average quantity of rain for each month.	Greatest quantity of rain recorded in one month.	Least quantity of rain recorded in one month.
	in.	in.	in.
January	1·68	4·83	0·30
February	1·58	3·69	0·04
March	1·61	3·45	0·40
April	1·73	4·79	0·06
May	1·96	4·16	0·50
June	1·83	4·26	0·59
July	2·37	6·65	0·10
August	2·40	4·65	0·07
September..............	2·40	4·79	0·40
October	2·67	5·37	0·53
November	2·53	4·33	0·85
December	2·02	4·72	0·08
Mean annual depth ...	24·781		

From the above synopsis, it appears that the greatest average quantity of rain falls in October and the least in February.

The heaviest rains, or those which yield the greatest quantity in the gauge, come down in the summer and early autumnal months. In the summer an inch and a half will sometimes fall in less than an hour in short but impetuous torrents; in the autumn the same quantity will occupy many hours in falling.

In winter the number of wet days exceeds that of the summer period; the average fall of a winter's rain is seldom more than $\frac{1}{10}$ of an inch an hour.

The amount of snow for the *thirty-four* years is included in the above Table.

Snow yields $\frac{1}{10}$ of water to 1 inch fall in depth; or a fall of snow of 10 inches in depth on the level would be equal to 1 inch of rain.

On the Vapour-Point.

The dew- or vapour-point is to many a subject involved in so much mystery, and hence apparently of so little importance in meteorological investigations, that very little attention has been practically bestowed upon the registration of connected series of observations; when it is viewed as a means of unfolding the state of the atmosphere with regard to its moisture and dryness, and therefore, as a means of assisting not only the floriculturist in the preservation of his exotics, but also each individual of the community in the protection of himself from the influences of a variable and humid climate, it will assume an interest which will overcome any supposed difficulty in its comprehension. The atmosphere derives its aqueous vapour from evaporation, and is lighter than air in the proportion of 1·000 to 0·625 : as evaporation is caused solely by heat, the quantity of vapour which any given portion of the atmosphere can contain must be dependent on the *temperature of the air* : Dalton's Table (page 36) of the elastic force of aqueous vapour, shows the quantity which can exist in it at every degree of temperature of Fahr. measured in the height of the mercurial column it can support. When the atmosphere is filled or saturated with vapour, if moisture be added, it will not increase the elasticity of the vapour already present, but it will collect into small drops and become visible in the form of mist or dew; the temperature at the moment of this collapse of the vapour into dew is called the dew- or vapour-point, by which, and our knowledge of the elasticity of vapour for each degree of temperature, we are enabled to ascertain with accuracy the quantity of vapour actually existing at any time in the atmosphere. If at the temperature of 50° objects be dewed with moisture, the elasticity of the vapour in the air is at its maximum ; it then supports 0·373 in. of the mercurial column, and the dew-point is 50°, the same temperature as the temperature of the air : if the temperature of the air should rise to 60°, the moisture would disappear, and the vapour might increase until its elasticity would support 0·523 in. of the mercurial column, when the temperature of the dew-point would again become the same as the temperature of the air, and moisture would be again deposited. As however the atmosphere is not always saturated with vapour, we must contrive, in order to ascertain the quantity in it, to bring the vapour it does contain to a maximum of elasticity, and force it to deposit moisture. This is effected by evaporation; the liquid, as it passes into vapour, abstracting the heat contiguous to the evaporating surface, to maintain itself in the vaporous form, reduces the temperature of the air until the vapour contained in it deposits dew; immediately the deposition takes place the dew-point is obtained; the temperature of evaporation must then be observed, and referring to Dalton's Table (page 36) we shall find under that temperature the elastic force of the vapour actually existing at that time in the atmosphere. The *higher* the temperature of the air the *greater* the quantity of vapour it can contain; if it approach saturation at a high temperature, its closeness and sultriness are oppressive; if, on the contrary, it be too dry, its harshness and chilliness are unpleasant to the sensations, as is experienced during the prevalence of the easterly winds in the spring months: the temperature at which *our* atmosphere is most frequently saturated, is rather below the mean of the climate. These different hygrometric states of the atmosphere afford a satisfactory explanation of the low temperatures of spring producing little moisture during the nights, while the heavy loaded vaporous atmosphere of autumn not only deposits copious dews, but originates the Stratus cloud and fogs. A Daniell's hygrometer gives the dew-point by inspection and requires no computation, but its manipulation is so delicate and good ether so difficult and expensive to purchase, that for popular use the wet and dry thermometer known as Mason's Hygrometer has been universally adopted *: the following Table and Rule will facilitate the reduction of the observations made with it.

* A very ingenious *organic* Hygrometer has been lately contrived by E. Simmons of Coleman Street; which shows approximately at *sight*, the dew-point, and relative humidity.

Table of Factors for deducing the Dew-point from the temperature of the air and the temperature of evaporation. (From the " Greenwich Magnetical and Meteorological Observations," 1844.)

Readings of the dry-bulb thermometer.	Factor.
Between 28° and 29°	5·7
... 29 ... 30	5·0
... 30 ... 31	4·6
... 31 ... 32	3·6
... 32 ... 33	3·1
... 33 ... 34	2·8
... 34 ... 35	2·6
... 35 ... 40	2·4
... 40 ... 45	2·3
... 45 ... 50	2·2
... 50 ... 55	2·1
... 55 ... 60	1·9
... 60 ... 70	1·8
... 70 ... 80	1·7
... 80 ... 85	1·6
... 85 ... 90	1·8

Rule.—Multiply the difference between the two thermometers by the *factor* corresponding to the temperature of the dry-bulb thermometer, and subtract the product from it; the remainder will be the temperature of the dew- or vapour-point.

$$\text{Let dry-bulb thermometer} = 66°$$
$$\text{Let wet-bulb thermometer} = 57$$
$$\text{Difference} = \overline{\ \ 9}$$
$$1·8$$
$$\text{Product} = \overline{16·2}$$
$$66° - 16°·2 = 49°·8 = \text{dew-point.}$$

The elasticity of vapour at the temperature of dew-point, $49°·8 = 0·372$ in.; the weight of a cubic foot of vapour at the temperature of dew-point, $49°·8 = 4·13$ grs.; but as the temperature of the air is $66°$, the elasticity of the vapour may increase to $0·638$ in.; and the weight of a cubic foot of vapour at $66°$ is $7·08$ grs.; therefore the air requires $2·95$ grs. more of vapour to become completely saturated with vapour.

The relative humidity of the air is found by considering complete saturation as *unity* or $1·000$.

In all other cases divide the number of grains of vapour contained in a cubic foot of air at dew-point, by the number of grains contained in a cubic foot at the temperature of the air; the quotient will always be *less* than unity.

In the above example $4·13$ grs. divided by $7·08$ grs. will give $0·583$ for the relative humidity.

To separate the gaseous from the aqueous pressure, subtract the elastic force of vapour at the temperature of the dew-point from the height of the mercurial column, the remainder will be the gaseous pressure.

in.

Reading of barometer . . . . . . $= 30·000$

Elastic force of vapour at $49°·8 =$ $0·372$

Gaseous pressure $= \overline{29·628}$

Note.—Dr. Apjohn's formula for finding dew-point is—

Above 32°.   Below 32°.

$$f'' = f' - \frac{d}{88} \times \frac{h}{30} \qquad\qquad f'' = f' - \frac{d}{96} \times \frac{h}{30}.$$

Where

f'' represents the force of aqueous vapour at temperature of dew-point.
f' represents the force of vapour at temperature of evaporation.
d represents the difference between dry and wet thermometers.
h height of barometer.

A Table showing the elastic force of aqueous vapour according to Dalton; and also the weight in grains Troy of a cubic foot of vapour as determined by Gay-Lussac for every degree of Fahrenheit from 0° to 90°.

Temperature. Fahrenheit.	Force of aqueous vapour.	Weight in grains Troy of cubic foot of vapour*.	Temperature. Fahrenheit.	Force of aqueous vapour.	Weight in grains Troy of cubic foot of vapour.	Temperature. Fahrenheit.	Force of aqueous vapour.	Weight in grains Troy of cubic foot of vapour.
	in.	gr.		in.	gr.		in.	gr.
0	0·061	0·78	37	0·238	2·80	64	0·597	6·65
5	·074	0·93	38	·246	2·89	65	·617	6·87
10	·089	1·11	39	·255	2·99	66	·638	7·08
12	·096	1·19	40	·264	3·09	67	·659	7·30
14	·104	1·28	41	·274	3·19	68	·681	7·53
15	·108	1·32	42	·283	3·30	69	·704	7·76
16	·112	1·37	43	·293	3·41	70	·727	8·00
17	·116	1·41	44	·304	3·52	71	·751	8·25
18	·120	1·47	45	·315	3·64	72	·776	8·50
19	·125	1·52	46	·326	3·76	73	·801	8·76
20	·129	1·58	47	·337	3·88	74	·827	9·04
21	·134	1·63	48	·349	4·01	75	·854	9·31
22	·139	1·69	49	·361	4·14	76	·882	9·60
23	·144	1·75	50	·373	4·28	77	·910	9·89
24	·150	1·81	51	·386	4·42	78	·940	10·19
25	·155	1·87	52	·400	4·56	79	0·970	10·50
26	·161	1 93	53	·414	4·71	80	1·001	10·81
27	·167	2·00	54	·428	4·86	81	1·034	11·41
28	·173	2·07	55	·442	5·02	82	1·067	11·47
29	·179	2·14	56	·458	5·18	83	1·101	11·82
30	·186	2·21	57	·473	5·34	84	1·135	12·17
31	·192	2·29	58	·489	5·51	85	1·171	12·53
32	·199	2·37	59	·506	5·69	86	1·208	12·91
33	·207	2·45	60	·523	5·87	87	1·247	13·29
34	·214	2·53	61	·541	6·06	88	1·286	13·68
35	·222	2·62	62	·559	6·25	89	1·326	14·08
36	·230	2·71	63	·578	6·45	90	1·369	14·50

* From the best authorities it is assumed that a cubic foot of dry air with a pressure of 30 inches and temperature of 32° of Fahrenheit weighs 563 grains.

* *The following Table and Theorem are from Sir George Shuckburgh, and will show how the Barometer is used for ascertaining the Height of Mountains.*

Explanation of Table I.

This Table gives the number of feet in a column of the atmosphere equivalent in weight to a like column of mercury $\frac{1}{10}$ of an inch high, when the barometer stands at 30 inches, for every 5 degrees of temperature ranging from 32° to 80°; and from this Table II. has been constructed as more convenient for general use :—

TABLE I.

Thermometer.	Feet.
32	86·85
35	87·49
40	88·54
45	89·60
50	90·66
55	91·72
60	92·77
65	93·82
70	94·88
75	95·93
80	96·99

TABLE II.

Thermometer.	Factor.	Thermometer.	Factor.	Thermometer.	Factor.
30	864·4	47	900·2	64	936·1
31	866·5	48	902·3	65	938·2
32	868·5	49	904·5	66	940·3
33	870·6	50	906·6	67	942·4
34	872·7	51	908·7	68	944·5
35	874·9	52	910·8	69	946·7
36	877·0	53	913·0	70	948·8
37	879·2	54	915·1	71	950·9
38	881·3	55	917·2	72	953·0
39	883·4	56	919·3	73	955·1
40	885·4	57	921·4	74	957·2
41	887·5	58	923·5	75	959·3
42	889·6	59	925·6	76	961·4
43	891·7	60	927·7	77	962·5
44	893·8	61	929·8	78	965·6
45	896·0	62	931·9	79	967·7
46	898·1	63	934·0	80	969·9

* To perform this operation accurately, two persons should take contemporary observations with two barometers and thermometers, the one at the bottom of the hill and the other at the top.

Rule.—Let

x = height of mountain required.

A = the mean height of the two barometers in inches.

a = the *difference* of the two.

b = the number in Table II. corresponding to the mean height of the two thermometers.

(Barometer at 30 inches.)

$$\text{Then } x = \frac{\overset{\text{in.}}{30}\, ab}{A}.$$

Example.—Suppose the barometer at the bottom of the mountain to stand at 30 inches, thermometer 60°; the barometer at the top 26·36 inches, thermometer 46°; required the height of the mountain, say Snowdon. The mean of the two barometers, or A, is 28·18 inches; their difference, or a, 3·64 inches; and the mean of the two thermometers, or b, 53°. In Table II. 913·0 is opposite to 53°; therefore

$$\frac{30 \times 3\cdot64 \times 913\cdot0}{28\cdot18} = 3538\cdot0 \text{ feet.}$$

A *Table of the velocities and pressures of the Wind.*

Miles per hour.	Force in lbs. on square foot.	
5	0·12	Gentle breeze.
10	0·49	} A brisk gale.
15	1·11	
20	1·97	Very brisk.
30	4·43	} High winds.
35	6·03	
40	7·87	} Very high.
45	9·96	
50	12·30	A storm.
60	16·71	A great storm.
80	31·49	} Tears up trees and destroys all before it.
100	49·20	

Depression of Mercury in glass tubes, or corrections to be added for capillary attraction.

Diameter of tube.	
in.	in.
0·25	0·020
0·30	0·015
0·40	0·007
0·45	0·005
0·60	0·002

Corrections for Temperature to be applied to Barometers mounted on brass scales.

Temp. of Fahr.	Inches. 24·5	Inches. 25·0	Inches. 25·5	Inches. 26·0	Inches. 26·5	Inches. 27·0	Inches. 27·5	Inches. 28·0	Inches. 28·5	Inches. 29·0	Inches. 29·5	Inches. 30·0	Inches. 30·5	Temp. of Fahr.
24	+·010	+·010	+·010	+·011	+·011	+·011	+·011	+·011	+·012	+·012	+·012	+·012	+·012	24
26	·006	·006	·006	·006	·006	·006	·006	·006	·006	·007	·007	·007	·007	26
28	+·001	+·001	+·001	+·001	+·001	+·001	+·001	+·001	+·001	+·001	+·001	+·001	+·001	28
30	-·003	-·003	-·004	-·004	-·004	-·004	-·004	-·004	-·004	-·004	-·004	-·004	-·004	30
32	·008	·008	·008	·008	·008	·008	·009	·009	·009	·009	·009	·009	·010	32
34	·012	·012	·013	·013	·013	·013	·014	·014	·014	·014	·015	·015	·015	34
36	·017	·017	·017	·017	·018	·018	·019	·019	·019	·020	·020	·020	·020	36
38	·021	·021	·022	·022	·023	·023	·023	·024	·024	·025	·025	·026	·026	38
40	·025	·026	·026	·027	·027	·028	·028	·029	·029	·030	·030	·031	·031	40
42	·030	·030	·031	·031	·032	·033	·033	·034	·034	·035	·036	·036	·037	42
44	·034	·035	·035	·036	·037	·037	·038	·039	·040	·040	·041	·042	·042	44
46	·038	·039	·040	·041	·042	·042	·043	·044	·045	·045	·046	·047	·048	46
48	·043	·044	·045	·045	·046	·047	·048	·049	·050	·051	·052	·052	·053	48
50	·047	·048	·049	·050	·051	·052	·053	·054	·055	·056	·057	·058	·059	50
52	·052	·053	·054	·055	·056	·057	·058	·059	·060	·061	·062	·063	·064	52
54	·056	·057	·058	·059	·060	·062	·063	·064	·065	·066	·067	·068	·070	54
56	·060	·061	·063	·064	·065	·066	·068	·069	·070	·071	·073	·074	·075	56
58	·064	·066	·067	·068	·070	·071	·073	·074	·075	·077	·078	·079	·081	58
60	·069	·070	·072	·073	·075	·076	·077	·079	·080	·082	·083	·085	·086	60
62	·073	·075	·076	·078	·079	·081	·082	·084	·085	·087	·088	·090	·091	62
64	·078	·079	·081	·083	·084	·086	·087	·089	·090	·092	·094	·095	·097	64
66	·082	·084	·085	·087	·089	·090	·092	·094	·096	·097	·099	·101	·102	66
68	·086	·088	·090	·091	·094	·095	·097	·099	·101	·102	·104	·106	·108	68
70	·091	·093	·095	·096	·098	·100	·102	·104	·106	·108	·109	·111	·113	70
72	·095	·097	·099	·101	·103	·105	·107	·109	·111	·113	·115	·117	·119	72
74	·099	·102	·104	·106	·108	·110	·112	·114	·116	·118	·120	·122	·124	74
76	·103	·106	·108	·110	·112	·114	·117	·119	·121	·123	·125	·127	·129	76
78	·108	·111	·113	·115	·117	·119	·122	·124	·126	·128	·130	·133	·135	78
80	-·114	-·115	-·117	-·119	-·122	-·124	-·126	-·129	-·131	-·133	-·136	-·138	-·140	80

Enter with approximate height of the barometer at the top of the table and the degree of the thermometer on the side of the page; then take out the correction with its proper sign.

Let barometer read . . 29·000
Correction . . . . - ·056
_____
Correct height for 32° 28·944

Thermometer attached = 50°

Corrections for Temperature to be applied to Barometers mounted in wood*.

Tempera-ture.	Inches. 28·5	Inches. 29·0	Inches. 29·5	Inches. 30·0	Inches. 30·5	Inches. 28·5	Inches. 29·0	Inches. 29·5	Inches. 30·0	Inches. 30·5	Tempera-ture.
25°	+·017	+·017	+·018	+·018	+·018	−·053	−·053	−·054	−·054	−·055	53°
26	·015	·015	·015	·015	·015	·055	·055	·056	·057	·058	54
27	·012	·012	·012	·012	·012	·056	·057	·058	·059	·060	55
28	·009	·010	·010	·010	·010	·059	·059	·060	·062	·063	56
29	·007	·007	·007	·007	·007	·062	·062	·062	·064	·065	57
30	·005	·005	·005	·005	·005	·064	·064	·065	·066	·067	58
31	·002	·003	·003	·003	·003	·066	·067	·068	·069	·071	59
32	+·000	+·000	+·000	+·000	+·000	·068	·069	·071	·072	·073	60
33	·002	·002	·002	−·002	−·003	·072	·072	·073	·074	·075	61
34	·005	·005	·005	·005	·005	·074	·074	·076	·077	·078	62
35	·007	·007	·008	·008	·008	·077	·077	·078	·080	·081	63
36	·010	·010	·011	·011	·011	·080	·080	·081	·083	·084	64
37	·013	·013	·013	·014	·014	·081	·082	·083	·085	·086	65
38	·015	·015	·015	·015	·015	·084	·085	·086	·087	·088	66
39	·018	·018	·018	·019	·019	·088	·088	·089	·090	·091	67
40	·020	·020	·020	·021	·021	·090	·090	·091	·093	·094	68
41	·023	·023	·023	·024	·024	·092	·092	·093	·095	·097	69
42	·025	·025	·025	·026	·026	·093	·094	·096	·098	·100	70
43	·028	·028	·028	·029	·030	·096	·097	·098	·100	·102	71
44	·030	·030	·030	·031	·032	·099	·099	·101	·103	·105	72
45	·032	·032	·033	·033	·034	·102	·102	·103	·106	·108	73
46	·035	·035	·036	·036	·036	·104	·105	·106	·108	·111	74
47	·037	·037	·038	·038	·038	·105	·107	·109	·112	·114	75
48	·039	·039	·040	·040	·040	·107	·109	·112	·115	·117	76
49	·041	·041	·043	·043	·043	·110	·112	·114	·117	·120	77
50	·044	·045	·046	·047	·047	·112	·114	·117	·120	·123	78
51	·047	·047	·049	·049	·050	·115	·117	·120	·123	·127	79
52	−·050	−·050	−·051	−·051	−·052	−·117	−·119	−·122	−·126	−·130	80

* The corrections in the above Table are due to the expansion of mercury only.

Enter at the top of the Table with the approximate height of the barometer, and on the left side of the page with the degree of the thermometer; take out the correction with its proper sign. In this Table all corrections above 32° are to be subtracted.

```
                              in.
Let barometer read  ...  29·500—therm. attached = 68°
Correction by Table ...  —·091
Correct height for 32°   29·409
```

Of the Sympiesometer.

The Sympiesometer, invented by Mr. Adie of Edinburgh, is a portable barometer used chiefly at sea, the motion of the ship rendering the mercurial column nearly useless in stormy weather : the principle of the instrument consists, in measuring the weight of the atmosphere, by the *compression* of a gaseous column; it consists of a tube terminating in a bulb above, and having the lower extremity bent upwards and expanding into an oval cistern open at the top : the bulb is filled with hydrogen gas, and a part of the cistern with a coloured fluid. The enclosed gas changes its bulk, or occupies more or less space according to the pressure of the atmosphere; but as the bulk is also altered by change of temperature, a correction must be applied on that account. For this purpose the principal or barometric scale is made to slide upon another scale, placed either below it, or on one side of it, which is divided into degrees and tenths, corresponding to the degrees of a common thermometer attached to the instrument; so as to represent the change of bulk in the gas produced by a change of temperature under the same pressure. When the Sympiesometer is hung up for observation, unturn the nut at the bottom, and then open the cistern by pushing up the small slider at its mouth; if any of the fluid at the top of the column should be separated, hang it up for a few minutes to drain, then turn it into a horizontal position, so that the fluid may run quickly up until the separated portion of it disappear, when it must be turned slowly upright. In using the instrument observe the temperature by the attached thermometer, and set the pointer *above* the top of the barometric or sliding scale opposite to the corresponding degree of temperature upon the fixed scale; the height of the *fluid,* as indicated on the *sliding* scale, will be the pressure of the atmosphere required. Suppose the temperature by attached thermometer to be 44°·5, then slide the barometric scale until its pointer be at 44°·5 on the fixed scale (it must be observed the numbers on this scale, as also those on the thermometer, read downwards); the top of the red fluid will mark the height of the barometer, which may be registered by the circular plate below, by turning the division on it corresponding to that indicated by the Sympiesometer, to the *fleur-de-lis.*

THE ANEROID BAROMETER.

The action of the *Aneroid* Barometer, lately invented by M. Vidi of Paris for ascertaining the variations of the atmosphere, depends on the effect produced by the pressure of the atmosphere on a metallic box from which the air has been exhausted and then hermetically sealed. It has already been explained that the weight of the column of the mercurial barometer is counterpoised by the weight of the atmosphere, and that the variations in the weight of the atmosphere are shown by the variations in the *length* of this column, and measured in inches and tenths; but in the Aneroid an index traversing a dial records the changes in the weight or *pressure* of the atmosphere on a *given surface,* suppose a square inch; it would therefore have greatly facilitated the comprehension of the action of the instrument had the dial been graduated to show the difference of the atmospheric pressure, in absolute weight or pounds. Though for purely scientific purposes the Aneroid is at present far removed from competition with the mercurial barometer, it nevertheless has some advantages in its extreme sensibility and its portability. Much has been urged against its variations from temperature; in a range from 28° to 80°, these seldom exceed a tenth of an inch; and it must be borne in mind, that if the mercurial barometer be subjected to the same range, it will be equally affected, only in the latter case the cause of the variation is satisfactorily established, and its exact amount for every degree of temperature accurately determined*. Of how little importance these variations are for the

---

* The perfect coincidence of the two instruments suggests the same corrections for temperature.

popular use of the Aneroid, the following observations will show.

Simultaneous observations of the Aneroid and Mercurial Barometer for the month of March 1848.

Date.	9 A.M.		Thermo-meter.	3 P.M.		Thermo-meter.
	Aneroid barometer.	Standard barometer.		Aneroid barometer.	Standard barometer.	
	in.	in.		in.	in.	
1.	28·66	28·67	50°	28·80	28·80	50°
2.	29·15	29·15	50	29·29	29·29	50
3.	29·88	29·90	48			
4.	30·12	30·14	46	30·11	30·12	51
5.	29·82	29·83	46	29·77	29·77	46
6.	29·87	29·88	46	29·84	29·85	47
7.	29·81	29·82	45			
8.	30·28	30·29	44	30·22	30·25	46
9.	29·98	29·99	49	29·89	29·90	52
10.	29·44	29·45	51	29·41	29·42	51
11.	28·91	28·93	50	28·84	28·85	50
12.	28·69	28·70	48	28·79	28·80	48
14.	29·76	29·78	47	29·85	29·88	49
15.	29·76	29·78	46	29·64	29 65	49
16.	29·49	29·50	48	29·49	29·49	49
17.	29·34	29·35	49	29·34	29·34	46
18.	29·44	29·45	46	29·37	29·37	52
19.	29·18	29·20	48	29·12	29·12	51
20.	28·98	28·99	48	28·97	28·98	49
21.	28·80	28·81	49	29·13	29·13	49
22.	29·60	29·60	47	29·67	29·68	51
23.	29·67	29·70	54	29·80	29·80	54
24.	30·02	30·02	55	30·10	30·10	55
25.	30·16	30·16	52	30·11	30·11	54
26.	29·89	29·90	53	29·80	29·80	54
27.	29·70	29·70	53	29·70	29·70	56
29.	29·91	29·91	54	29·91	29·90	56
30.	29·81	29·80	55	29·81	29·80	58
31.	29·98	29·98	58	30·00	30·00	65

The next series of observations, showing the portability of the Aneroid for measuring heights, and also its convenience as a meteorological barometer, were taken during an excursion into Wales in the summer of 1848.

London to Chester (*viâ* Trent Valley) Stations.	Readings of the Aneroid Barometer.
August 10th.	in.
Davies Street, Berkeley Square.....................	30·05
Harrow station	29·85
Tring (highest ground)	29·71
Cheddington	29·82
Wolverton	29·89
Blisworth...	29·78
Weedon	29·83
Rugby	29·82
Atherstone	29·90
Norton Bridge.......................................	29·90
Chester, St. Peter's Churchyard	30·11
August 11th.	
Railway viaduct over the Dee at Chester	30·14
Upon a hill on the coach-road from Ruabon to Llangollen	29·69
Llangollen Bridge	29·91

Llangollen is assumed to be about 200 feet higher than the Estuary of the Dee near Chester.

Elevations. August 12, 13 and 18.		Before going out	Return home
		at Llangollen.	
	in.	in.	in.
Castle Dinas Bran.................................	29·02	29·92	29·90
Rising ground to S. of Barber's Hill	28·75	29·87	29·81
A high hill S.W. of Llangollen, 2 miles, and marked down in Ordnance Map *Grouse Box*	28·24	29·89	29·70
Very high ground west of *Grouse Box* and leading to *Moel Ferna*, situated in *Berwyn Chain*	28·02	29·89	29·70

Journal of the Weather at Llangollen, Denbighshire.

1848.	Aneroid barometer, 9 A.M.	Therm. in shade, 9 A.M.	Aneroid barometer, 3 P.M.	Therm. in shade, 3 P.M.	Aneroid barometer, 9 P.M.	Thermometer, 9 P.M.	Wind.	Weather, &c.
Aug.	in.	°	in.	°	in.	°		
12.	29·92	62	29·90	64	...	...	N.W.	Fair.
13.	29·87	59	...	65	29·81	...	E.S.E.	Ditto; evening cloudy.
14.	29·76	52	29·74	51	29·72	50	E.	Incessant rain.
15.	29·77	55	29·76	60	29·75	...	E.	Cloudy.
16.	29·70	55	29·70	67	29·72	58	S.E.	Fair; heavy rain all night.
17.	29·65	57	29·68	59	29·85	49	E.	Rain and wind till 8 P.M.
18.	29·89	61	29·70	57	29·58	57	S.S.E.	Fine A.M.; evening and night
19.	29·51	59	29·58	62	29·62	56	W.	Fine. [incessant heavy rain.
20.	29·73	63	29·75	64	29·76	58	S.W.	*Nimbi*; rain in torrents at night.
21.	29·195	52	(29·09—)*	57	29·32	54	W.	Destructive tempest, with
22.	29·35	...	29·36	...	...	...	W.	Showery. [small rain.
23.	29·51	...	29·58	59	...	58	W.	Heavy showers; lightning and
24.	29·77	...	...	...	...	...	W.	Heavy showers. [rain at night.
25.	...	...	29·87	...	...	...	W.	Fine.

16. A brilliant parhelion, seen to the right of the sun about 6 P.M. The *true* sun behind a mountain, in a cloud.

21. This storm exceeded any on record since January 1839; many hundred trees were either partly or wholly destroyed; the spray of the river Dee at *Llangollen* was, during some of the most violent gusts, carried higher than the adjacent houses, and the noise of the waters resembled the roar of thunder.

22. The Dee much swollen; the waters rush down their rocky bed with impetuosity.

* About the *minimum* point, which continued for 3 *hours*. By temporary gauge, the quantity of rain fallen estimated at 5 inches for the 14 days.

Journal of the Weather at Hastings.

1848.	9 A.M.		9 P.M.		Wind.	
Aug.31.	...	°	30·20	60°	N.E.	Fine. Lightning to s.w. & N.E. evening and night.
Sept. 1.	30·31	...	30·42	52	E.N.E.	Fine.
2.	30·55	...	30·56	60	W.N.W.	*Cumuli*; calm; very fine.
3.	30·56	...	30·52	58	...	Dead calm and clear; sea perfectly still.
4.	30·39	...	30·22	...	S.E.	Clear.
5.	30·05	...	29·96	66	S.	Fine; appearance of thunder to s.w.
6.	30·03	...	30·17	59	W.	A breeze; *scud*; fine night.
7.	30·22	...	30·22	61	W.S.W.	Clear day succeeded by a cloudy night.
8.	30·18	60	...	...	W.	Cloudy.

Sept. 6. Near the windmill on the in.
top of Fairlight Down 29·44 ⎫ Temperature
Reading—before going out 30·03 ⎬ about 65°.
Reading—return home ... 30·07 ⎭

On the 8th of September the instrument was again
suspended in its usual place at Greenwich, and it was
found that the *zero-point* had remained perfectly steady.

Simultaneous observa-
tions made during
the Winter of 1849.

1849.	Aneroid Barometer.	Standard Barometer.	Thermom.
	in.	in.	°
Jan. 18.	30·00	30·001	60
20	30·31	30·315	67
21.	30·29	30·293	64
23.	30·38	30·379	57
24.	30·34	30·342	62
25.	30·14	30·135	58
26.	29·91	29·910	60
27.	29·63	29·640	62
28.	29·40	29·401	55
29	30·10	30·100	56
Feb. 4.	30·50	30·502	61
11.	30·85	30·840	55
...	30·93	30·915	59
Mar. 29.	29·42	29·425	54

Reading of the Aneroid taken
on the Caledonian Railway,
and between Preston and
Carlisle.

1849.		in.
Aug. 3.	At Lanark	29·51
	Near Elvanfoot Station (near the Lowther Hills)	29·11
	Carlisle Station	30·17
	Shap Station	29·30
	Near Morecombe Bay	30·18

Rise of the line of road between
Carlisle and Elvanfoot nearly 1000
feet.

In consulting the above journals, we find that the movements of the Aneroid were always consistent. It was a delightful companion, and highly useful, its indications preventing many an excursion which would have ended in disappointment. The tourist should never travel without it; and the seaman will find it a safe guide when the motion of the mercurial column renders the marine barometer almost useless. In all cases the writer has *used* the Aneroid as its inventor intended it *should be used*; and its movements are so far perfect, that they merit the calm and impartial investigation of the *true* philosopher, whose vocation is to aid the development of ingenuity, and not to crush its efforts because they are not perfection.

The two following diagrams are by Mr. Redwood, and the explanation of the Aneroid is nearly the same as that communicated by the same gentleman to the Pharmaceutical Society.

Fig. 1.

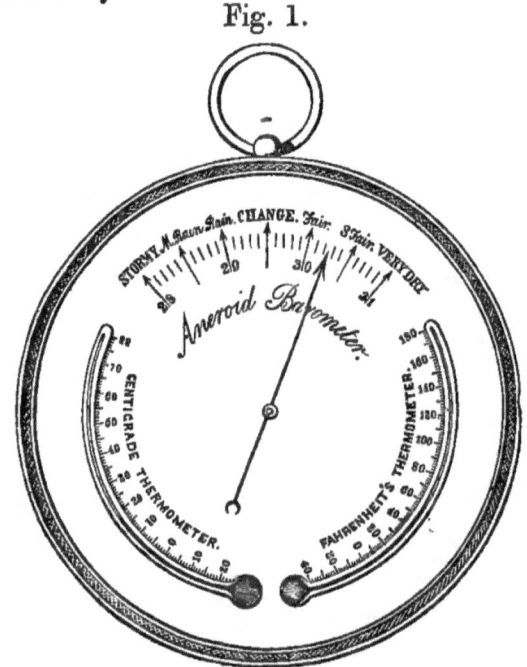

Fig. 1 represents the external appearance of the instrument. It is four inches and three-quarters in diameter across the face, and one inch and three-quarters
in thickness. The pressure of the atmosphere is indicated by a hand pointing to a scale, which is graduated
to correspond with the common barometer: thermometers are placed on the face, one of which is essential.

Fig. 2.

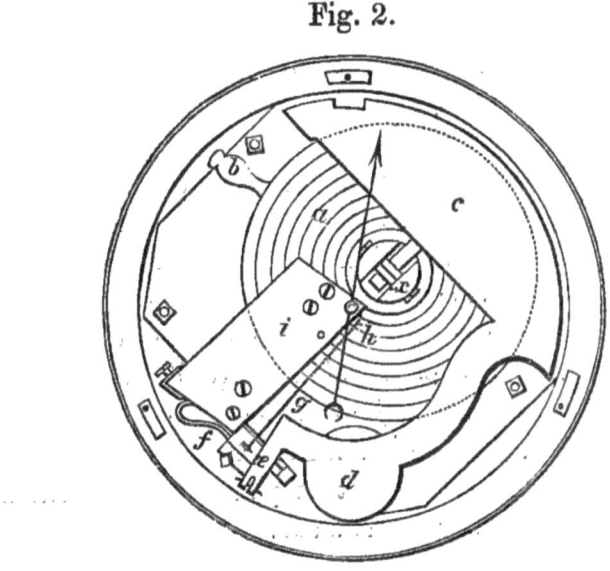

Fig. 2 represents the internal construction as seen
when the face is removed, but with the hand still attached. *a* is a flat circular box made of some white
metal, exhausted of air through the short tube *b*, which
is subsequently made air-tight by soldering: the upper
and lower surfaces of the box are corrugated in concen-
tric circles, which gives it greater elasticity; and the
box is fixed to the bottom of a metallic case, which in-
closes the mechanism of the whole instrument. In the
centre of the *upper* surface of the elastic box is a solid

cylindrical socket *x*, about half an inch high, to the top of which the *principal lever*, *c*, *d*, *e*, is attached; this lever, which brings the box into a state of tension by separating the surfaces, rests partly on a spiral spring *d*, and partly on two fulcrums having knife-edges, with perfect freedom of motion; the end *e* of the large or principal lever is attached to a second lever *f*, from which a fine watch-chain *g* extends to *h*, where it works on a drum attached to the arbour of the hand; a hair spring at *h*, the attachments of which are made to the metallic plate *i*, regulates the motion of the hand.

As the weight of the atmosphere is increased or diminished, so is the surface of the corrugated elastic box depressed or elevated, as is also at the same time the spiral spring *d*, upon which the principal lever rests; and this motion is communicated through the levers to the arbour of the hand at *h*. The tension of the box in its construction is equal to 44 lbs. At the back of the Aneroid is a screw to adjust the hand to the height of any standard mercurial barometer : for comparative observations the Aneroid must be placed in the position for which the adjustment is made.

A perspective view of the interior of the Aneroid.

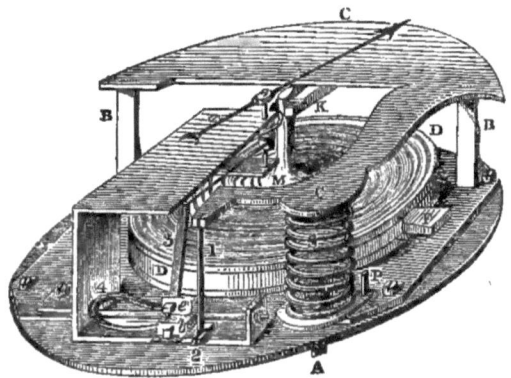

A. Screw adjusting the hand.
BB. Fulcrums.
CC. Principal Lever.
DD. Vacuum vase.
1. Vertical rod connecting lever CC with levers 2 and 3.
e b. Adjusting screws for leverage.
S. Spiral spring.
M. Socket in vacuum vase.
K. Pin attached to socket.

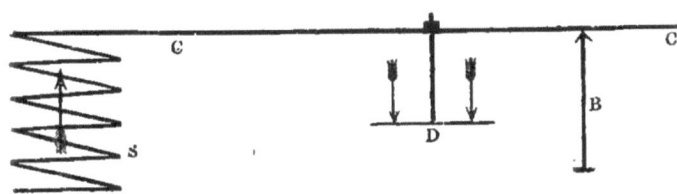

D. Vacuum vase (the arrows indicate the downward
    pressure of the atmosphere).
C. Principal lever.
B. Fulcrum.
S. Spring.

The height of the Atmosphere being assumed at 27·500 feet, with the Barometer at 30·00 inches and the Thermometer at 55° of Fahrenheit, the following Table of Elevations has been computed, answering to the corresponding depressions of the mercury in the Barometer.

Height of the barometer.	Feet.	Height of the barometer.	Feet.
in.		in.	
30·0	0	27·3	2592
29·9	92	27·2	2692
29·8	184	27·1	2793
29·7	276	27·0	2895
29·6	368	26·9	2997
29·5	462	26·8	3099
29·4	556	26·7	3201
29·3	650	26·6	3304
29·2	744	26·5	3406
29·1	838	26·4	3511
29·0	933	26·3	3615
28·9	1028	26·2	3719
28·8	1123	26·1	3824
28·7	1219	26·0	3926
28·6	1315	25·0	5000
28·5	1411	24·0	6111
28·4	1508	23·0	7263
28·3	1605	22·0	8462
28·2	1702	21·0	7907
28·1	1799	20·0	11000
28·0	1897	19·0	12345
27·9	1996	18·0	13750
27·8	2095	17·0	15214
27·6	2194	16·0	16740
27·5	2392	15·0	18335
27·4	2491	10·0	27500

The following rule, which gives results very near the truth, will be useful in deducing elevations from the Aneroid.

As the *sum* of the readings of the barometer or Aneroid is to their *difference*, so is 55·000 (or twice the assumed height of the atmosphere in feet) to the elevation required.

To find the height of Fairlight Down near Hastings,

$$
\begin{array}{ll}
\text{Let the reading of the Aneroid on the Marine Parade, Hastings} \Big\} = 30{\cdot}05 & \begin{array}{l} 30{\cdot}05 \\ 29{\cdot}44 \end{array} \\[2ex]
\text{\ldots \quad \ldots \quad at the bottom of the windmill on the Down} \Big\} = 29{\cdot}44 & \overline{\quad 0{\cdot}61} = \text{difference.}
\end{array}
$$

$$\text{Sum} \ldots \ = 59{\cdot}49$$

$$\therefore \ \ 59{\cdot}49 : 0{\cdot}61 :: 55{\cdot}000 : 564 \text{ nearly.}$$

The Table of elevations computed by the above formula at the temperature of 55°, and the lower barometer at 30 inches, may be found interesting to those who may wish to see at a glance the heights corresponding to the depressions of the barometer.

Thus on the Grampian Hills a depression of 4 inches gives an elevation of 4000 feet; at the crater of Mount Etna a depression of 10 inches gives 11,000 feet; and on the summit of the mountains of Thibet, supposed the loftiest in the world, a depression of 20 inches gives an elevation of 27,500.

INDEX.

THE END.